Ryu Uchiyama

# REPTILES AND AMPHIBIANS

5          FUJI  RVP

5          36▷5A

CHRONICLE BOOKS

SAN FRANCISCO

**02** Red-Eyed Tree Frog │ *AGALYCHNIS CALLIDRYAS*

**03** Gliding Leaf Frog | *AGALYCHNIS SPURRELLI*

**04** White's Tree Frog │ *LITORIA CAERULEA*

**06** Strawberry Poison Dart Frog │ *Dendrobates pumilio*

**09** Helmeted White-Chinned Frog | *POLYPEDATES OTILOPHUS*

**10a** | Cranwell's Horned Frog

**10b** | Painted-Belly Monkey Frog

**15** Ornate Horned Frog | *CERATOPHRYS ORNATA*

**19a** | Spotted Salamander
*AMBYSTOMA MACULATUM*

**19b** | Boulenger's Oriental Salamander
*HYNOBIUS BOULENGERI*

Madagascar Velvet Gecko │ *HOMOPHOLIS BOIVINI*

**21** Taylor's Gecko | *GEKKO TAYLORI*

| *Teratoscincus scincus*

**27a** | Nosy Be Flat-Tail Gecko
*Uroplatus ebenaui*

**27b** | Lined Flat-Tail Gecko
*Uroplatus lineatus*

Asian Water Dragon | *PHYSIGNATHUS COCINCINUS*

**29**  Blacktail Toadhead Agama | *PHRYNOCEPHALUS MACULATUS*

| *HELODERMA SUSPECTUM*

**33** New Caledonian Giant Crested Gecko | *RHACODACTYLUS CILIATUS*

**34** Humphead Forest Dragon | *GONOCEPHALUS* SP.

**35** Humphead Forest Dragon | *GONOCEPHALUS* SP.

Baja California Rock Lizard | *PETROSAURUS THALASSINUS*

Smooth Helmeted Iguana │ *CORYTOPHANES CRISTATUS*

**43** Many-Colored Bush Anole | *POLYCHRUS MARMORATUS*

Short-Horned Lizard │ *PHRYNOSOMA DOUGLASSII*

**45** Bearded Dragon │ *POGONA VITTICEPS*

| *TILIQUA SCINCOIDES*

Australian Frilled Lizard | *CHLAMYDOSAURUS KINGII*

**49** Panther Chameleon | *FURCIFER PARDALIS*

Flapneck Chameleon │ *CHAMAELEO DILEPIS*

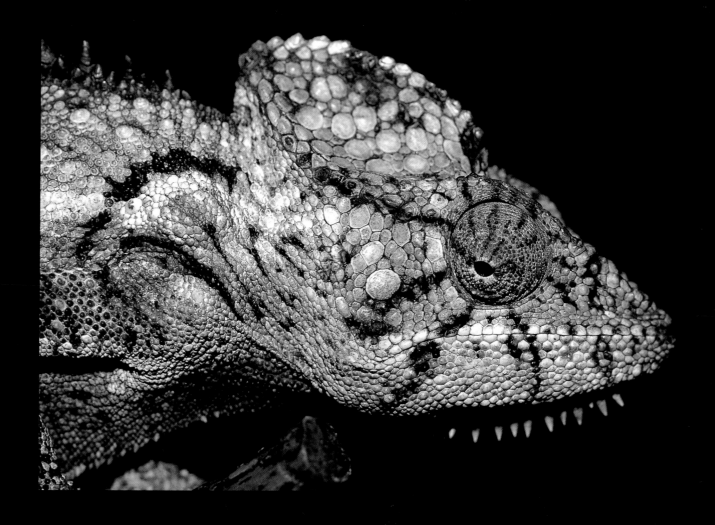

Oustalet's Chameleon | *FURCIFER OUSTALETI*

**53a** Veiled Chameleon | *CHAMAELEO CALYPTORATUS*

**53b** Parson's Chameleon | *CALUMMA PARSONII*

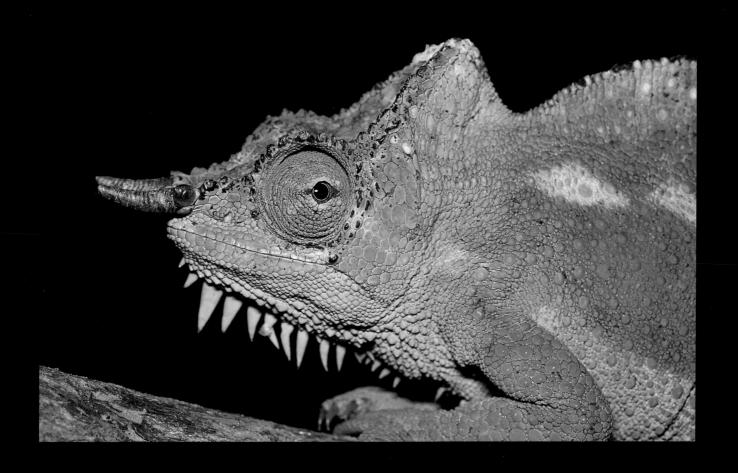

**55** Four-Horned Chameleon | *CHAMAELEO QUADRICORNIS*

**56a** Temple Pit Viper | *TROPIDOLAEMUS WAGLERI*

**56b** Temple Pit Viper | *TROPIDOLAEMUS WAGLERI*

Emerald Tree Boa | *CORALLUS CANINUS*

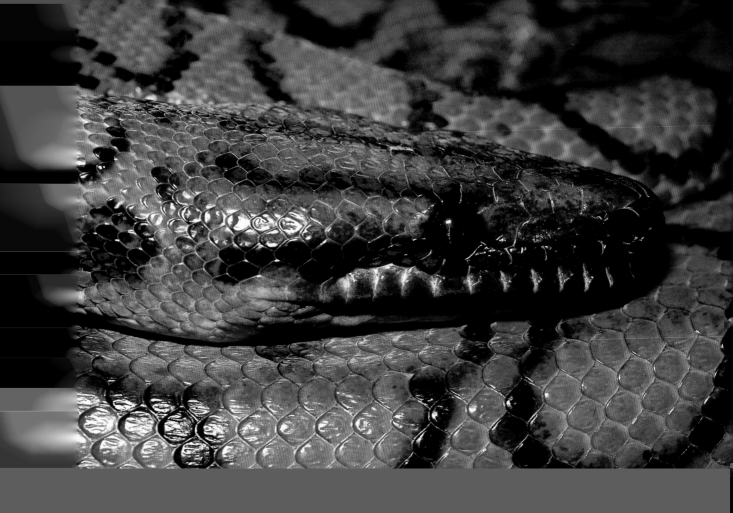

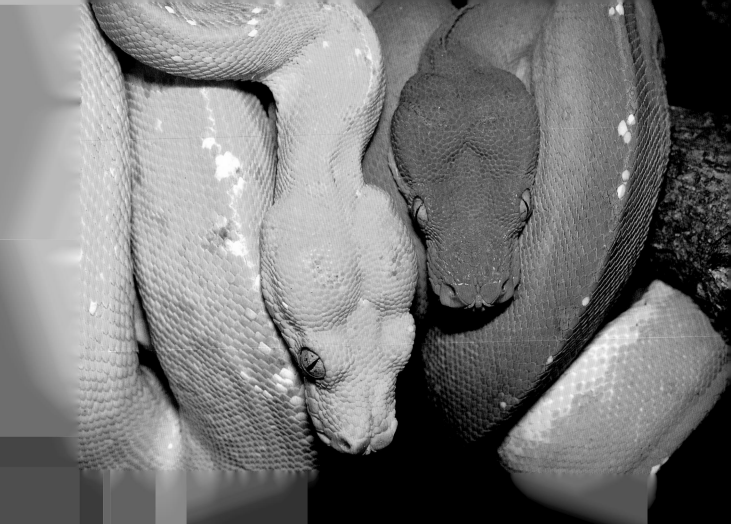

**68a** | Schokari Sand Racer
*PSAMMOPHIS SCHOKARI*

**68b** | Hooded Snake
*MACROPROTODON CUCULLATUS CUCULLATUS*

**72a** | Chiapas Giant Musk Turtle
_STAUROTYPUS SALVINII_

**72b** | Pig-Nosed Turtle
_CARETTOCHELYS INSCULPTA_

**72c** | Wattle-Necked Softshell Turtle
_PALEA STEINDACHNERI_

**72d** | Siebenrock's Snakeneck Turtle
_CHELODINA SIEBENROCKI_

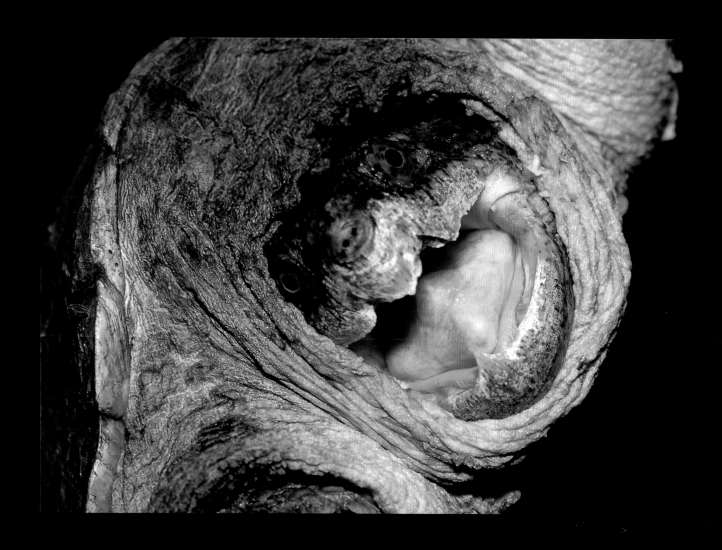

| *MACROCLEMYS TEMMINCKII*

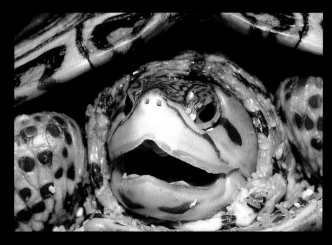

**75a** | Loggerhead Musk Turtle
*Kinosternon minor*

**75b** | Diamondback Terrapin
*Malaclemys terrapin*

**75c** | Yellow Pond Turtle
*Mauremys mutica*

**75d** | Spotted Turtle
*Clemmys guttata*

Mexican Giant Musk Turtle │ *STAUROTYPUS TRIPORCATUS*

**77** Reimann's Snakeneck Turtle | *CHELODINA REIMANNI*

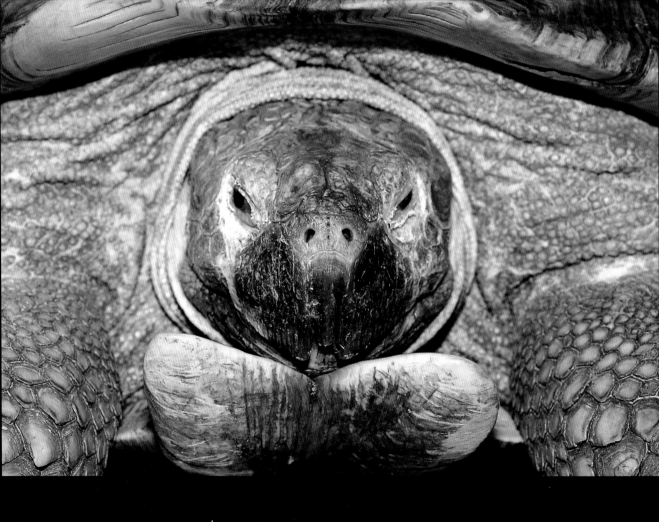

| *GEOCHELONE SULCATA*

Red-Eared Slider | *TRACHEMYS SCRIPTA ELEGANS*

| *RHINOCLEMMYS PULCHERIMA MANNI*

**83** Schneider's Smooth-Fronted Caiman | *PALEOSUCHUS TRIGONATUS*

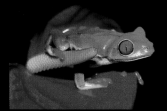
**02** **Red-Eyed Tree Frog**
*AGALYCHNIS CALLIDRYAS*

**03** **Gliding Leaf Frog**
*AGALYCHNIS SPURRELLI*

**04** **White's Tree Frog**
*LITORIA CAERULEA*

**05** **Java Whipping Frog**
*POLYPEDATES LEUCOMYSTAX*

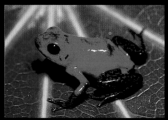
**06** **Strawberry Poison Dart Frog**
*DENDROBATES PUMILIO*

**07** **Tomato Frog**
*DYSCOPHUS ANTONGILII*

**08** **Thai Spadefoot Toad**
*LEPTOBRACHIUM HENDRICKSONI*

**09** **Helmeted White-Chinned Frog**
*POLYPEDATES OTILOPHUS*

**10a** **Cranwell's Horned Frog**
*CERATOPHRYS CRANWELLI*

**10b** **Painted-Belly Monkey Frog**
*PHYLLOMEDUSA SAUVAGEI*

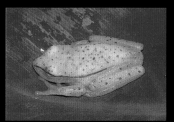
**11** **Polka-Dot Tree Frog**
*HYLA PUNCTATA*

**12** **Surinam Toad**
*PIPA PIPA*

**13** **Asian Horned Toad**
*MEGOPHRYS NASUTA*

**14** **Budgett's Frog**
*LEPIDOBATRACHUS LAEVIS*

**15** **Ornate Horned Frog**
*CERATOPHRYS ORNATA*

**16** **African Clawed Frog**
*XENOPUS LAEVIS*

**17** **Mexican Axolotl**
*AMBYSTOMA MEXICANUM*

**18** **Alta Verapaz Salamander**
*BOLITOGLOSSA DOFLEINI*

**19a** **Spotted Salamander**
*AMBYSTOMA MACULATUM*

**19b** **Boulenger's Oriental Salamander**
*HYNOBIUS BOULENGERI*

**20** **Madagascar Velvet Gecko**
*HOMOPHOLIS BOIVINI*

**21** **Taylor's Gecko**
*GEKKO TAYLORI*

**22** **Madagascar Ground Gecko**
*PAROEDURA PICTUS*

**23** **Tokay Gecko**
*GEKKO GECKO*

**24** **Southern Flat-Tail Gecko**
*UROPLATUS SIKORAE*

**25** **Golddust Day Gecko**
*PHELSUMA LATICAUDA*

**26** **Common Wonder Gecko**
*TERATOSCINCUS SCINCUS*

**27a** **Nosy Be Flat-Tail Gecko**
*UROPLATUS EBENAUI*

**27b** **Lined Flat-Tail Gecko**
*UROPLATUS LINEATUS*

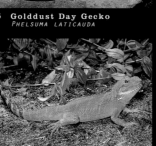

**28** **Asian Water Dragon**
*PHYSIGNATHUS COCINCINUS*

**29** **Blacktail Toadhead Agama**
*PHRYNOCEPHALUS MACULATUS*

**30** **Gila Monster**
*HELODERMA SUSPECTUM*

**31 Komodo Dragon**
*VARANUS KOMODOENSIS*

**32 Crocodile Skink**
*TRIBOLONOTUS SP.*

**33 New Caledonian Giant Crested Gecko**
*RHACODACTYLUS CILIATUS*

**34 Humphead Forest Dragon**
*GONOCEPHALUS SP.*

**35 Humphead Forest Dragon**
*GONOCEPHALUS SP.*

**36 Plumed Basilisk**
*BASILISCUS PLUMIFRONS*

**37 Rhinoceros Iguana**
*CYCLURA CORNUTA*

**38 Desert Monitor**
*VARANUS GRISEUS*

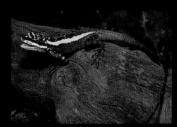

**39 Agamidae**

**40 Solomon Island Skink**
*CORUCIA ZEBRATA*

**41 Baja California Rock Lizard**
*PETROSAURUS THALASSINUS*

**42 Smooth Helmeted Iguana**
*CORYTOPHANES CRISTATUS*

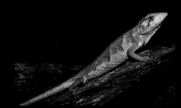

**43 Many-Colored Bush Anole**
*POLYCHRUS MARMORATUS*

**44 Short-Horned Lizard**
*PHRYNOSOMA DOUGLASSII*

**45 Bearded Dragon**
*POGONA VITTICEPS*

**46 Eastern Blue-Tongued Skink**
*TILIQUA SCINCOIDES*

**47** Australian Frilled Lizard
*CHLAMYDOSAURUS KINGII*

**48-49** Panther Chameleon
*FURCIFER PARDALIS*

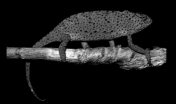

**50** Flapneck Chameleon
*CHAMAELEO DILEPIS*

**51** Oustalet's Chameleon
*FURCIFER OUSTALETI*

**52** Antsingy Leaf Chameleon
*BROOKESIA PERARMATA*

**53a** Veiled Chameleon
*CHAMAELEO CALYPTORATUS*

**53b** Parson's Chameleon
*CALUMMA PARSONII*

**54** Fischer's Chameleon
*BRADYPODION FISCHERI*

**55** Four-Horned Chameleon
*CHAMAELEO QUADRICORNIS*

**56a** Temple Pit Viper
*TROPIDOLAEMUS WAGLERI*

**56b** Temple Pit Viper
*TROPIDOLAEMUS WAGLERI*

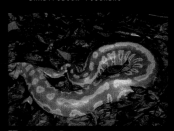

**57** Blood Python
*PYTHON CURTUS*

**58** Black-Headed Cat Snake
*BOIGA NIGRICEPS*

**59** Northern Leafnose Snake
*LANGAHA MADAGASCARIENSIS*

**60** Boelen's Python
*MORELIA BOELENI*

**61** Emerald Tree Boa
*CORALLUS CANINUS*

**62  Rainbow Water Snake**
*ENHYDRIS SP.*

**63  Japanese Rat Snake**
*ELAPHE CLIMACOPHORA*

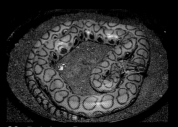

**64  Rainbow Boa**
*EPICRATES CENCHRIA CENCHRIA*

**65  Burmese Python**
*PYTHON MOLURUS BIVITTATUS VAR.*

**66  Green Tree Python**
*MORELIA VIRIDIS*

**67  Green Tree Python**
*MORELIA VIRIDIS*

**68a  Schokari Sand Racer**
*PSAMMOPHIS SCHOKARI*

**68b  Hooded Snake**
*MACROPROTODON CUCULLATUS
CUCULLATUS*

**69  Sunbeam Snake**
*XENOPELTIS UNICOLOR*

**70  Snakeneck Turtle**
*CHELODINA SP.*

**71  New Guinea Snapping Turtle**
*ELSEYA NOVAEGUINEAE*

**72a  Chiapas Giant Musk Turtle**
*STAUROTYPUS SALVINII*

**72b  Pig-Nosed Turtle**
*CARETTOCHELYS INSCULPTA*

**72c  Wattle-Necked Softshell Turtle**
*PALEA STEINDACHNERI*

**72d  Siebenrock's Snakeneck Turtle**
*CHELODINA SIEBENROCKI*

**73  American Snapping Turtle**
*CHELYDRA SERPENTINA*

**74 Alligator Snapping Turtle**
*MACROCLEMYS TEMMINCKII*

**75a Loggerhead Musk Turtle**
*KINOSTERNON MINOR*

**75b Diamondback Terrapin**
*MALACLEMYS TERRAPIN*

**75c Yellow Pond Turtle**
*MAUREMYS MUTICA*

**75d Spotted Turtle**
*CLEMMYS GUTTATA*

**76 Mexican Giant Musk Turtle**
*STAUROTYPUS TRIPORCATUS*

**77 Reimann's Snakeneck Turtle**
*CHELODINA REIMANNI*

**78 African Spurred Tortoise**
*GEOCHELONE SULCATA*

**79 Galapagos Tortoise**
*GEOCHELONE NIGRITA*

**80 Red-Eared Slider**
*TRACHEMYS SCRIPTA ELEGANS*

**81 Painted Wood Turtle**
*RHINOCLEMMYS PULCHERIMA MANNI*

**82 American Alligator**
*ALLIGATOR MISSISSIPPIENSIS*

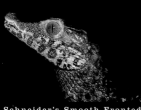

**83 Schneider's Smooth-Fronted
Caiman**
*PALEOSUCHUS TRIGONATUS*

**02** Red-Eyed Tree Frog
*AGALYCHNIS CALLIDRYAS*
$2-2^3/_4$ INCHES (5-7 CM)
*Central America*
Females of this common and colorful rainforest frog fill their eggs with water from their bladders to keep the jelly-like eggs from becoming too dry.

**03** Gliding Leaf Frog
*AGALYCHNIS SPURRELLI*
$2^3/_4-4^1/_2$ INCHES (7-9 CM)
*Central America*
This frog spreads its webbed toes to form a parachute as it glides from tree to tree.

**04** White's Tree Frog
*LITORIA CAERULEA*
$2^3/_4-4^1/_2$ INCHES (7-11 CM)
*Australia, New Guinea,
   introduced to New Zealand*
Larger than most tree frogs, White's can control how much water escapes through its skin. A thick fold of skin behind the head gives this frog a plump look. When startled, it makes a piercing scream.

**05** Java Whipping Frog
*POLYPEDATES LEUCOMYSTAX*
$2-2^3/_4$ INCHES (5-7 CM)
*Southeast Asia*
A mating pair spends all night whipping up a frothy nest of foam for newly laid eggs. Foam nests can be made on emerging plants, tree stumps, or concrete and metal structures in villages and cities.

**06** Strawberry Poison Dart Frog
*DENDROBATES PUMILIO*
$^3/_4-1$ INCH (1.8-2.4 CM)
*Central America*
The bright colors and bold behavior of this frog warn other animals that its skin carries a deadly toxin. After her eggs hatch, a female carries each of the young separately on her back to a safe place where the tadpoles mature.

**07** Tomato Frog
*DYSCOPHUS ANTONGILII*
$2^1/_2-4$ INCHES (6-10 CM)
*Madagascar*
Though found in few parts of Madagascar, this frog's size, color, and call make it well known there. To defend itself, the tomato frog puffs up its body with air or emits a noxious secretion.

**08** Thai Spadefoot Toad
*LEPTOBRACHIUM HENDRICKSONI*
$1^1/_2-2^1/_2$ INCHES (4-6 CM)
*Thailand*
Males of some species have a row of spines above the mouth, which may be used in aggression.

**09** Helmeted White-Chinned Frog
*POLYPEDATES OTILOPHUS*
$2^1/_2-4$ INCHES (6-10 CM)
*Borneo and Sumatra*
Both males and females have broad disks on their toe tips, but only males possess nuptial pads to help them grasp females beneath the arms during mating. With their legs, the frogs whip up a nest of foam over a pond, into which tadpoles drop when they are ready.

**10a** Cranwell's Horned Frog
*CERATOPHRYS CRANWELLI*
$2^3/_4-4^3/_4$ INCHES (7-12 CM)
*South America*
With its big mouth and strong jaws, this frog lunges and bites in defense. Its appetite extends to other frogs, which it lures close by raising a hindfoot and wriggling its toes. Even the tadpoles are carnivores, equipped with a serrated beak.

**10b** Painted-Belly Monkey Frog
*PHYLLOMEDUSA SAUVAGEI*
$2^1/_4-3^1/_2$ INCHES (5.5-8.5 CM)
*Argentina*
To keep from drying out, this frog secretes a waxy substance from glands on its head and rubs the wax all over its skin with its back legs.

**11 Polka-Dot Tree Frog**
*HYLA PUNCTATA*
$1^1/_4$–$1^1/_2$ INCHES (3–4 CM)
*Amazon Basin, South America*
With its big white eyes that appear to
pop from its head, this spotted tree frog
can inflate a throat sac to call attention
to itself when it wants to find a mate.

**12 Surinam Toad**
*PIPA PIPA*
4–$6^3/_4$ INCHES (10–17 CM)
*South America*
This flat, odd-looking toad courts and
mates underwater. During an acrobatic
dance, the male presses fertilized eggs
onto his mate's back. The eggs stay there
for a few months until the babies hatch
and swim away.

**13 Asian Horned Toad**
*MEGOPHRYS NASUTA*
$2^3/_4$–$5^1/_2$ INCHES (7–14 CM)
*Southeast Asia*
Its coloration and the fleshy horns on its
eyes and snout make this toad look just
like a leaf on the rainforest floor, helping
it escape the notice of predator or prey.

**14 Budgett's Frog**
*LEPIDOBATRACHUS LAEVIS*
$4^1/_2$–$4^3/_4$ INCHES (11–12 CM)
*Paraguay*
Tadpoles mature in temporary ponds,
and cannibalism among young siblings
sometimes occurs.

**15 Ornate Horned Frog**
*CERATOPHRYS ORNATA*
4–$4^3/_4$ INCHES (10–12 CM)
*Argentina, Brazil, and Uruguay*
Often buried beneath leaves and moss in
the rainforest, the horned frog waits to
grab and gulp prey with its wide mouth.
Its name comes from the pointy ridges
above its eyes.

**16 African Clawed Frog**
*XENOPUS LAEVIS*
$3^1/_4$–4 INCHES (8–10 CM)
*Native to Africa but widely
introduced elsewhere*
This frog's tadpoles suspend themselves
in water from an egg capsule by a thread
of mucus until they grow a usable mouth
and tail. Then they join a school of tadpoles
that stay in mid-water by fluttering their
tails.

**17 Mexican Axolotl**
*AMBYSTOMA MEXICANUM*
$7^1/_2$–10 INCHES (18–25 CM)
*Mexico*
This salamander of plateau lakes never
grows up, because adults retain the exter-
nal gills (seen behind the head) of a juve-
nile. This phenomenon, called neoteny,
occurs in other *AMBYSTOMA* salamanders.

**18 Alta Verapaz Salamander**
*BOLITOGLOSSA DOFLEINI*
6–8 INCHES (15–20 CM)
*Mexico*
Lacking lungs, this salamander breathes
through its skin. It has webbed feet and a
prehensile tail. Males have two bumps of
skin on the upper lip.

**19a Spotted Salamander**
*AMBYSTOMA MACULATUM*
6–8 INCHES (15–20 CM)
*Eastern North America, from Nova
Scotia and Ontario to Texas*
Most of its life takes place underground,
but after heavy rain, the spotted salamander emerges to locate pools of water,
where it mates.

**19b Boulenger's Oriental
Salamander**
*HYNOBIUS BOULENGERI*
$6^1/_2$–8 INCHES (16–20 CM)
*Eastern Asia*
Protective males of this primitive salamander genus guard eggs deposited in water
against any intruders, except other
females with more eggs. Each hind foot
has only four toes.

**20 Madagascar Velvet Gecko**
*HOMOPHOLIS BOIVINI*
10–12 INCHES (25–30 CM)
*Madagascar*
Active by day, this gecko sticks to a
territory that it occupies with its mate.

**21 Taylor's Gecko**
*GEKKO TAYLORI*
$9^1/_2$-$11^1/_4$ INCHES (24-28 CM)
*Thailand*
Like many large geckos, Taylor's makes a lot of noise. This species has only recently been described by researchers.

**22 Madagascar Ground Gecko**
*PAROEDURA PICTUS*
$4^3/_4$-6 INCHES (12-15 CM)
*Madagascar*
Many Madagascan geckos prefer clinging to trees, but this one sticks to the ground. It occurs commonly in the dry forest and thorn scrub in the west and south of the island.

**23 Tokay Gecko**
*GEKKO GECKO*
10-14 INCHES (25-35 CM)
*Southeast Asia, India, and south China*
Named for its harsh-sounding call that carries for a hundred yards, the temperamental tokay gecko clings to crevices inside homes. It hunts insects, rodents, and small lizards.

**24 Southern Flat-Tail Gecko**
*UROPLATUS SIKORAE*
6-$7^1/_4$ INCHES (15-18 CM)
*Madagascar*
This big-eyed gecko has a leaf-shaped tail and broad skin flaps that help it to blend in with tree bark. Members of this genus can grow to more than a foot long.

**25 Golddust Day Gecko**
*PHELSUMA LATICAUDA*
4-$5^1/_4$ INCHES (10-13 CM)
*Madagascar and Comoro Islands*
Besides the gold specks, this gecko can also be recognized by the blue rim above its eye and its yellow throat. A rare blue mutant also occurs. The lizard's special toe pads let it cling to walls or banana leaves.

**26 Common Wonder Gecko**
*TERATOSCINCUS SCINCUS*
6-$6^3/_4$ INCHES (15-17 CM)
*Central Asia, Iran, and*
*Arabian peninsula*
Waving its tail sideways rubs its scales together and causes a hissing sound that serves as this gecko's defense. It lays fragile, hard-shelled eggs, which can better withstand the dry desert than the leathery eggs of most lizards.

**27a Nosy Be Flat-Tail Gecko**
*UROPLATUS EBENAUI*
$2^1/_2$-$3^1/_4$ INCHES (6-8 CM)
*Madagascar*
This species relies less on skin flaps for camouflage than its close relatives, but it does have "horns" of skin above its eyes.

**27b Lined Flat-Tail Gecko**
*UROPLATUS LINEATUS*
$7^1/_4$-10 INCHES (18-25 CM)
*Madagascar*
Found in bamboo forests, the lined flat-tail gecko also shows few extra fringes or flaps of skin. Note the tiny skin spines behind each eye.

**28 Asian Water Dragon**
*PHYSIGNATHUS COCINCINUS*
2-3 FEET (60-90 CM)
*Southern Asia*
This lizard can run upright on its hind legs to get out of danger. If it happens to be basking on a branch over a river, though, it will plop into the water and swim somewhere safe.

**29 Blacktail Toadhead Agama**
*PHRYNOCEPHALUS MACULATUS*
$5^1/_4$-6 INCHES (13-15 CM)
*Central Asia to China*
*and northern India*
Shuffling its body through sand to build burrows, this squat desert lizard protects its eyes with thick, tight-closing lids and a projecting brow.

**30 Gila Monster**
*HELODERMA SUSPECTUM*
$9^1/_4$-20 INCHES (23-50 CM)
*Southwestern United States*
*and northern Mexico*
One of the world's two venomous lizards, the Gila monster uses its venom to subdue birds, young rodents, and rabbits. Its eggs develop for ten months before hatching.

**31 Komodo Dragon**
*VARANUS KOMODOENSIS*
6½–10 FEET (200–300 CM)
*Komodo and three other
Indonesian islands*
Up to ten feet long and weighing 300
pounds, no lizard gets bigger than the
Komodo dragon. A scavenger and hunter
of deer and pigs, the dragon has also, on
occasion, killed and eaten people.

**32 Crocodile Skink**
*TRIBOLONOTUS SP.*
4–9½ INCHES (10–24 CM)
*Solomon Islands and New Guinea*
Small, shy, and spiny, this moist forest
dweller raises its body and tail when
alarmed and gives a high-pitched yelp.
The crocodile skink is a strong swimmer,
swaying its body sideways like its larger
namesake.

**33 New Caledonian
Giant Crested Gecko**
*RHACODACTYLUS CILIATUS*
4–9½ INCHES (10–24 CM)
*New Caledonia, Isle of Pines*
This genus includes the world's largest
gecko and a range of reproduction from
laying soft-shelled and hard eggs to
giving birth to live young. *RHACODACTYLUS*
spends all its time in trees. This species
was thought to be extinct for more than
100 years, until it was rediscovered in
1994. Its color can vary from brown and
yellow to even a shade of blue.

**34 & 35 Humphead Forest Dragon**
*GONOCEPHALUS SP.*
10 INCHES (25 CM)
*Indochina, Malaysia, Indonesia,
the Philippines, Australia*
This large, tree-dwelling agamid lizard
displays a spiny crest down its back. In
Australia, three *GONOCEPHALUS* species
live in the northern rainforests.

**36 Plumed Basilisk**
*BASILISCUS PLUMIFRONS*
2–2½ FEET (60–70 CM)
*Central America*
A habit of sprinting across the surface of
water on its hind legs earned this species
the nickname "Jesus Christ Lizard." Only
males possess the prominent double crest
on the head.

**37 Rhinoceros Iguana**
*CYCLURA CORNUTA*
3⅓–4 FEET (100–120 CM)
*Haiti, Dominican Republic*
Like its namesake, this lizard has horns
on its snout, skin folds on its throat, and
is extremely rare. It stays on the ground
and eats insects, berries, and plants.

**38 Desert Monitor**
*VARANUS GRISEUS*
4–4⅔ FEET (120–140 CM)
*Northern India west through Caspian
region to North Africa*
An open-country hunter of rodents,
lizards, and snakes, one monitor can distinguish another's age and sex from scent
trails left on the ground. When a male
encounters a female's scent trail, he will
turn and follow it.

**39 Agamidae**
4–4⅔ FEET (120–140 CM)
*Africa, Australia, Asia, and Europe*
About 300 species comprise the family of
agamid lizards, similar to iguanas but
found throughout the Old World. Males of
some African species have bright blue
heads that they bob in courtship displays,
when they also appear to perform push-
ups atop rocks.

**40 Solomon Island Skink**
*CORUCIA ZEBRATA*
4–4⅔ FEET (120–140 CM)
*Solomon Islands*
More than two feet long, this heavy, slow-
moving skink rarely comes down from the
trees. Good thing that it's an herbivore,
the only skink with that diet.

**41 Baja California Rock Lizard**
*PETROSAURUS THALASSINUS*
10–12 INCHES (25–30 CM)
*Baja California, Mexico*
This agile climber leaps between rocks but
explores open country to find flowers,
berries, and leaves to eat. Blue heads and
brighter colors distinguish lizards found
closer to the tip of the Baja peninsula.

**42 Smooth Helmeted Iguana**
*CORYTOPHANES CRISTATUS*
1–2 FEET (30–35 CM)
*Mexico to northwest Colombia*
Named for the neck crest it erects to face
off an adversary, this iguana actually
prefers to rely on camouflage and slow
movements to protect itself from predators. It eats large insects.

**43 Many-Colored Bush Anole**
*POLYCHRUS MARMORATUS*
10–12 INCHES (25–30 CM)
*Amazon Basin and Venezuela*
Though not true chameleons, these noc-
turnal iguana relatives are commonly
referred to as the chameleons of the
Americas because of their ability to
change color.

**44 Short-Horned Lizard**
*PHRYNOSOMA DOUGLASSII*
$2^1/_2$–$5^1/_2$ INCHES (6–14 CM)
*Southern Canada to Southwestern
    United States and Pacific Northwest*
This species lives in cooler areas than
other horned lizards but ranges from dry
prairies to mountaintop conifer forests.
The genus name means "toad-bodied," and
these lizards are often called horned "toads."

**45 Bearded Dragon**
*POGONA VITTICEPS*
16–18 INCHES (40–45 CM)
*Australia*
An inflatable throat sac armed with
spiny scales gives the dragon its name
and provides its main defense. A gaping
mouth exposes a yellow lining.

**46 Eastern Blue-Tongued Skink**
*TILIQUA SCINCOIDES*
1–2 FEET (30–60 CM)
*Australia*
When threatened, this stocky skink rolls
out its bright blue tongue to distract the
intruder. Its omnivorous diet includes
fruits, leaves, insects, and snails.

**47 Australian Frilled Lizard**
*CHLAMYDOSAURUS KINGII*
2–3 FEET (60–90 CM)
*Australia*
When unfurled, its wrap-around frill
creates the illusion of a much larger
adversary. When not needed, the frill
stays folded flat around the neck.

**48 & 49 Panther Chameleon**
*FURCIFER PARDALIS*
16–20 INCHES (40–50 CM)
*Madagascar and Réunion*
Males display an array of shades and have
the ability to change color quickly, while
females are pinkish brown. It occurs in the
scrubby habitat of northeast Madagascar.

**50 Flapneck Chameleon**
*CHAMAELEO DILEPIS*
10–12 INCHES (25–30 CM)
*African tropical region to South Africa*
Chameleons need sharp vision to capture
prey with sticky tongues as long as their
bodies. All chameleons are considered
threatened by habitat loss.

**51 Oustalet's Chameleon**
*FURCIFER OUSTALETI*
$1^1/_3$–2 FEET (40–60 CM)
*Madagascar*
Two-thirds of all chameleons come from
Madagascar, and this is the world's
largest. It can be found in villages and
even cities.

**52 Antsingy Leaf Chameleon**
*BROOKESIA PERARMATA*
$3^1/_2$–$4^1/_2$ INCHES (9–11 CM)
*Madagascar*
Leaf chameleons tend to be small, spiny,
and earth-toned. This one grows twice as
large as some species, but still is only four
inches long.

**53a** Veiled Chameleon
*CHAMAELEO CALYPTORATUS*
$1^1/_3$-2 FEET (40-60 CM)
*Yemen*
The impressive helmet-like casque on its head can reach two inches high. It has been rumored to collect dew on high, dry plateaus where the chameleon lives, but more likely serves as a weapon.

**53b** Parson's Chameleon
*CALUMMA PARSONII*
$1^1/_2$-2 FEET (45-60 CM)
*Madagascar*
Nearly the largest chameleon, Parson's reaches two feet long and prefers humid rainforests. As this photo shows, chameleon eyes move independently, and can rotate up to 180 degrees.

**54** Fischer's Chameleon
*BRADYPODION FISCHERI*
10-14 INCHES (25-35 CM)
*Tanzania and Kenya*
Known for aggressive displays, this chameleon stabs rivals with its broad horn. Chameleons rarely leave the trees except to court or to lay eggs in a deep burrow.

**55** Four-Horned Chameleon
*CHAMAELEO QUADRICORNIS*
10-14 INCHES (25-35 CM)
*Cameroon*
Most horned chameleons have three or fewer horns, but this species has an extra one. Not true horns, they are flexible growths from scales and can ram rivals or help a lizard recognize others of its kind.

**56a & b** Temple Pit Viper
*TROPIDOLAEMUS WAGLERI*
$1^2/_3$-$2^2/_3$ FEET (50-80 CM)
*Southeast Asia*
This snake relies on infrared-sensing pits between its eyes and mouth and a prehensile tail to hunt from trees. Its color changes with age from green to black with yellow spots and bars.

**57** Blood Python
*PYTHON CURTUS*
$6^1/_2$-9 FEET (200-270 CM)
*Southeast Asia, Indonesia*
A stout, chunky hunter, the blood python lies in wait for passing prey. Females protect their eggs for two months until they hatch.

**58** Black-Headed Cat Snake
*BOIGA NIGRICEPS*
5-$5^3/_4$ FEET (150-170 CM)
*Southern Asia and nearby islands*
Named for its vertical pupil and its nighttime prowling through trees, cat snakes use both venom and constriction to subdue prey such as lizards or birds, which are often swallowed head first.

**59** Northern Leafnose Snake
*LANGAHA MADAGASCARIENSIS*
2-$2^2/_3$ FEET (60-80 CM)
*Madagascar*
Slender as a twig, this snake sports a strange, scaly extension to its snout—pointy on males and leaf-shaped on females. Males also have a distinct white line along their bodies.

**60** Boelen's Python
*MORELIA BOELENI*
6-8 FEET (180-240 CM)
*New Guinea*
Found in high-altitude rain forests, Boelen's python has special protection in Papua New Guinea. Heat-sensitive pits can be seen between scales alongside the mouth.

**61** Emerald Tree Boa
*CORALLUS CANINUS*
$3^1/_2$-6 FEET (100-180 CM)
*South America*
Pitted scales along the jaw help this rain forest canopy hunter detect small mammals and lizards to eat. This boa and the unrelated green tree python show convergent evolution of size, shape, and behavior.

**62** Rainbow Water Snake
*ENHYDRIS SP.*
20 INCHES (50 CM)
*China, India, Southeast Asia, Australia, New Guinea*
Valved nostrils and watertight scales adapt this species to an aquatic life. Grooves at the base of the teeth may help to grasp and pierce fish scales.

**63** Japanese Rat Snake
*ELAPHE CLIMACOPHORA*
$3^1/_2$-$6^1/_2$ FEET (100-200 CM)
*Japan*
The rat snake swallows large eggs after crushing the shell with spines projecting down from its backbones. A naturally albino population in Japan has been protected as a national treasure.

**64** Rainbow Boa
*EPICRATES CENCHRIA CENCHRIA*
5-6$^1$/$_2$ FEET (150-200 CM)
*Brazil*
This small boa sparkles with an iridescent sheen. It hunts small mammals and birds and suffocates them with the crushing coils of its body.

**65** Burmese Python
*PYTHON MOLURUS BIVITTATUS VAR.*
12-20 FEET (360-600 CM)
*Pakistan, India, Sri Lanka east through southern Asia*
The albino or "golden" form of this boa comes from selective captive breeding. Burmese pythons can reach nearly 20 feet long, though 12 feet is a more common limit.

**66 & 67** Green Tree Python
*MORELIA VIRIDIS*
5$^1$/$_2$-6 FEET (160-180 CM)
*New Guinea*
While resting in the rainforest canopy, the python drapes the coils of its body evenly over a branch. Mating occurs in a similar position, with tails intertwined. A mix of skin pigments creates a snake's color. A layer of reflecting particles combines with a layer of yellow skin cells to produce the green color that lets the python blend in with leaves.

**68a** Schokari Sand Racer
*PSAMMOPHIS SCHOKARI*
2$^1$/$_3$-4$^2$/$_3$ FEET (70-130 CM)
*Africa and Middle East*
Perhaps to seal their scales or spread their scent, these curious snakes rub a secretion from their nostrils along their entire body. They are capable of short sprints up to 7 miles per hour, and if captured will spin rapidly until their tail breaks off.

**68b** Hooded Snake
*MACROPROTODON CUCULLATUS CUCULLATUS*
1-2 FEET (30-60 CM)
*Southwest Europe, North Africa, and the Near East*
This seldom-seen snake is active at night and prefers to eat lizards.

**69** Sunbeam Snake
*XENOPELTIS UNICOLOR*
2$^2$/$_3$-4 FEET (80-120 CM)
*Southeast Asia*
One of two species in an ancient family of burrowing snakes, the sunbeam snake rarely appears above ground to show off its sparkling scales. Hinged teeth fold back to let prey pass down the throat, then lock in place to block escape.

**70** Snakeneck Turtle
*CHELODINA SP.*
6 INCHES (15 CM)
*Australia and New Guinea*
Eight species comprise this semi-aquatic genus of turtles, distinguished by a long, thick neck and flat, oval shell. Some release a strong odor or foul-smelling liquid from skin glands.

**71** New Guinea Snapping Turtle
*ELSEYA NOVAEGUINEAE*
10-12 INCHES (25-30 CM)
*New Guinea*
Juveniles have a dark brown shell, which turns black in adults. This turtle occurs in much of New Guinea but prefers coastal rivers and swamps.

**72a** Chiapas Giant Musk Turtle
*STAUROTYPUS SALVINII*
8-10 INCHES (20-25 CM)
*Mexico, El Salvador, Guatemala*
The male has rough scales on its hind legs to help him cling to the female during mating, especially when she bites his jaw.

**72b** Pig-Nosed Turtle
*CARETTOCHELYS INSCULPTA*
1$^2$/$_3$-2$^1$/$_3$ FEET (50-70 CM)
*Australia and New Guinea*
Though found in fresh water, the pig-nosed turtle resembles a small sea turtle with its paddle-like forelimbs. The thick snout and flared nostrils resemble a pig's.

**72c  Wattle-Necked Softshell
Turtle**
*PALEA STEINDACHNERI*
12-16 INCHES (30-40 CM)
*China southwest to Vietnam,
introduced to Hawaii*
Named for a clump of rough tubercles
at the base of the neck, this turtle's head
and neck stripes will fade with age. Adults
rarely bask, but young turtles come ashore
to soak up sun.

**72d  Siebenrock's Snakeneck
Turtle**
*CHELODINA SIEBENROCKI*
10-12 INCHES (25-30 CM)
*New Guinea*
This carnivore spends most of its time
buried in mud, awaiting a meal. It springs
at prey with a neck three-fourths the
length of its shell. It lives in brackish
streams and swamps.

**73  American Snapping Turtle**
*CHELYDRA SERPENTINA*
14-18 INCHES (35-45 CM)
*North, Central and South America,
from Canada to Ecuador*
This famously foul-tempered turtle has
strong jaws and sturdy legs. It stays on
the bottom of ponds and eats insects,
plants, fish, birds, and amphibians.

**74  Alligator Snapping Turtle**
*MACROCLEMYS TEMMINCKII*
$1^2/_3$-$2^2/_3$ FEET (50-80 CM)
*Mississippi Valley and southeastern
United States*
This ancient species looks like some fossil
beast with its knobby, serrated shell and
hooked beak. Foraging by night, it eats
whatever it catches—frogs, crustaceans,
even other turtles. It can lure fish into its
mouth by wriggling a worm-like "lure" of
flesh in the middle of its tongue.

**75a  Loggerhead Musk Turtle**
*KINOSTERNON MINOR*
$2^3/_4$-$4^1/_2$ INCHES (7-11 CM)
*Southeastern United States*
Juveniles eat insects and plants, but the
extra crushing surface on the jaws allows
adults to eat more hard-shelled mollusks.
This turtle mates underwater in shady,
hidden places, such as by a fallen tree.

**75b  Diamondback Terrapin**
*MALACLEMYS TERRAPIN*
8-$9^1/_4$ INCHES (20-23 CM)
*Atlantic and Gulf coasts of the
United States, Florida Keys*
A resident of coastal marshes, tidal flats,
and lagoons, this turtle scavenges, and
sometimes hunts, snails, mollusks, and
crustaceans.

**75c  Yellow Pond Turtle**
*MAUREMYS MUTICA*
6-$6^3/_4$ INCHES (15-17 CM)
*Vietnam, southern China, Hainan,
and Taiwan*
Fond of low-elevation ponds, this turtle
feeds on fish and likes to bask in the sun.

**75d  Spotted Turtle**
*CLEMMYS GUTTATA*
4-$4^3/_4$ INCHES (10-12 CM)
*Southern Ontario south to Florida
and west to Illinois*
The namesake spots are transparent
patches in the shell that expose yellow
pigment below. At home in water or
ashore, one or more males will chase a
female in both places until she concedes
to mate.

**76  Mexican Giant Musk Turtle**
*STAUROTYPUS TRIPORCATUS*
12-$14^3/_4$ INCHES (30-37 CM)
*Mexico, Belize, Guatemala, and
Honduras*
The broad head and jutting snout help
this voracious predator capture fish,
amphibians, and even smaller turtles.

**77  Reimann's Snakeneck Turtle**
*CHELODINA REIMANNI*
$7^1/_4$-8 INCHES (18-20 CM)
*South-central New Guinea*
These side-necked turtles have a special
vertebrae structure that allows them to
bend their long necks sideways to pull
their head into their shell.

**78** African Spurred Tortoise
*GEOCHELONE SULCATA*
2-2¹/₂ FEET (60-75 CM)
*Senegal east to Ethiopia and Sudan*
The world's largest mainland tortoise, it survives along the southern edge of the Sahara Desert by being active at dusk or dawn and digging burrows to escape the heat. It relies on moisture in food for much of its water.

**79** Galapagos Tortoise
*GEOCHELONE NIGRITA*
3¹/₃-4¹/₃ FEET (100-130 CM)
*Santa Cruz Island, Galapagos*
Several tortoise species evolved on the Galapagos Islands, and each has a particular shell shape or other distinctive feature. When not grazing on grass or eating cactus pads, this tortoise might soak in a mud hole.

**80** Red-Eared Slider
*TRACHEMYS SCRIPTA ELEGANS*
8-11¹/₄ INCHES (20-28 CM)
*Mississippi Valley from Illinois to the Gulf Coast*
With fourteen subspecies, this is the most variable turtle known, as well as a popular pet. A courting male strokes the female's face with his foreclaws, then climbs on top of her so both sink to the bottom of a pond, where they mate.

**81** Painted Wood Turtle
*RHINOCLEMMYS PULCHERIMA MANNI*
7¹/₄-8 INCHES (18-20 CM)
*Nicaragua, Costa Rica*
No other turtle matches the colorful palette of this subspecies. It becomes active after rains and enjoys wading or swimming in streams.

**82** American Alligator
*ALLIGATOR MISSISSIPPIENSIS*
13¹/₂-20 FEET (400-600 CM)
*Southeastern United States from North Carolina to Texas*
With big powerful jaws and bony armor along its back and tail, the alligator is a fearsome resident of southern swamps and marshes. Females construct nests built of mud, humus, and vegetation to incubate their eggs.

**83** Schneider's Smooth-Fronted Caiman
*PALEOSUCHUS TRIGONATUS*
4³/₄-5³/₄ FEET (140-170 CM)
*Orinoco and Amazon basins from Venezuela and Guiana to southern Brazil*
Clear streams with waterfalls and rapids are this reptile's haunt. Its thick, armored belly protects it from being killed for its skin.

# "You look very funny!"

That was my reaction the first time I looked at a reptile through the viewfinder of my camera. I was simply surprised because, until then, most of my photographs had been of fish. From reptiles, however, I began to sense something different from fish. Everything about reptiles was very fresh to me and I wanted to photograph as many different species as possible. I also tried to take pictures of their entire bodies, as in illustrated guidebooks. When I laid out these pictures, I realized that they lacked the charm that had first fascinated me. How could I capture the fresh impact that hit me at my first encounter?

After much thought, I came to realize that, for small-sized creatures, their major worry is being attacked by predators. A bird is a good example of a predator, attacking them from the sky. Accordingly, small-sized creatures seem to instinctively react to an attack from above. I had one particular experience that explains this well. I was once taking pictures of some reptiles and when the lighting cast the camera's shadow on them, they started scurrying around as if going mad. I was astonished by what happened. They must have thought that a predator was after them. Then an idea hit me and I lowered the camera little by little until it reached their eye level. It was not until I lay on my stomach with the camera touching the ground that I felt I was succeeding in having a tête-à-tête talk with them.

Once I reached that point, taking pictures of reptiles and amphibians was no longer work. It was rather as if I were enjoying conversations with them, or playing with them. Some reptiles and amphibians looked dull or frightening, and others had very unusual shapes or colors. It was hard to believe that a world of such interesting creatures existed. Every time I looked into the viewfinder, there was a new discovery, joy after joy. I was fortunate in a way because I had little knowledge of reptiles and amphibians. Little knowledge meant little preconception. The impact I received was directly passed on to the film. Photography is a very curious art. It seems the photographer's feelings are faithfully transferred to the film. When I press the shutter thinking **"How cute you are!"** a cute picture will turn out. If I am saying, **"Don't bite me!"** the picture will show my fear.

In Japanese, "photograph" is aptly written in two characters: the first character means "to copy or to reproduce" and the second "truth or fact or real thing." That is exactly how this book is. This is not a mere illustrated guide to reptiles and amphibians. It is a

> > >

collection of intimate portraits of them. In each picture I took there was much enjoyment.

In order to complement my little knowledge of reptiles and amphibians, I asked many people for information. I thank them for their generous and willing help. Most of the reptiles and amphibians in this book were photographed in specialty pet shops and in zoos. A few were taken in their natural habitats. I am grateful to all those people who made available not only animals but also places for photographing them. Special thanks to those reptiles and amphibians whom I surprised with a strong strobe light. I hope they will forgive me, since I intended no harm.

**Ryu Uchiyama** was born in Tokyo in 1962. He is a graduate of the Department of Fisheries of Tokai University's School of Marine Science and Technology. As he was drawn to the study of ancient fish, his interest extended to the evolutionary process in general of vertebrates and then to reptiles and amphibians. He became a devoted photographer of them. He is the author and co-author of eleven guidebooks on fish and reptiles, all published in Japan.

Photography equipment used for the photographs in
this book:

OLYMPUS OM-4 CONTAX RTS-III
HASSELBLAD 553ELX
ZUIKO MACRO 90MM, F2 MACRO PLANAR T*60MM,
    F2.8 MACRO PLANAR CF 120MM, F4 MACRO
    PLANAR T*100MM, F2.8

FILMS ARE ALL FUJICHROME BELVIA.

First published in the United States in 1999
    by Chronicle Books.
First published in Japan in 1997
    by Heibonsha Limited, Publishers.
Copyright © 1997 by Ryu Uchiyama.
Printed in Hong Kong.
ISBN 0-8118-2306-7
Library of Congress Cataloging-in-Publication Data
available.

TEXT AND COVER DESIGN: Anne Galperin
COVER PHOTOGRAPH: Ryu Uchiyama
ORIGINAL DESIGN: Tsuyokatsu Kudo
CAPTIONS: Blake Edgar
TRANSLATION (AFTERWORD): Isao Tezuka

Distributed in Canada by
Raincoast Books
8680 Cambie Street
Vancouver, B.C. V6P 6M9

10 9 8 7 6 5 4 3 2

Chronicle Books
85 Second Street
San Francisco, California 94105

www.chroniclebooks.com